A Letter for Tiger

Janosch, geboren 1931 in Zaborze, Oberschlesien, arbeitete in
verschiedenen Berufen, ab 1953 als freier Künstler. Er lebt und arbeitet
auf einer einsamen Insel. Seine Kinder- und Bilderbücher erscheinen bei
Beltz & Gelberg und weltweit in vielen Übersetzungen.
In englischer Sprache liegen von Janosch in der Reihe MINIMAX außerdem
die Bilderbücher *The Trip to Panama* und *Little Tiger, Get Well Soon!* vor.

Didaktisches Begleitmaterial zu diesem Titel finden Sie
als Download unter www.beltz.de/lehrer

Herausgegeben in Zusammenarbeit mit dem Moritz Verlag
von Markus Weber

www.beltz.de
Erstmals als MINIMAX bei Beltz & Gelberg im Februar 2007
© 1980, 1982 Beltz & Gelberg
in der Verlagsgruppe Beltz · Weinheim Basel
Alle Rechte vorbehalten
Ausgabe des Bilderbuchs *Post für den Tiger* in englischer Sprache
für die deutschsprachigen Länder
© der englischen Übersetzung bei Andersen Press Ltd., London
Gesamtherstellung: Beltz Bad Langensalza GmbH, Bad Langensalza
Printed in Germany
ISBN 978-3-407-76046-3
5 6 7 8 9 15 14

A Letter for Tiger

Translated by Anthea Bell

One day, when Little Bear was setting off to go
fishing in the river again, Little Tiger said:

»Bear, I feel so lonely when you're away. I wish you'd write a letter home, to cheer me up. Please do!«

»All right,« said Little Bear, and he took a bottle of blue ink with him. He also took a canary's feather, because you can write very well with a canary quill pen.

He took some notepaper too, and an envelope for his letter.

When he was down by the riverside, first he put a worm on his hook, and then he put the hook and line in the water, and then he picked up the quill pen and wrote a letter on the notepaper, in blue ink. It said:

---

to cheer someone up: jemanden aufmuntern
canary quill pen: Kanarienvogelfeder
hook: Haken

»Dear Tiger,
This is to let you know that I am very well. How
are you? Please peel the onions and boil the
potatoes while I'm out.

I may bring home a fish for supper. With love and kisses from Little Bear.«

Then he put the letter in the envelope and stuck it up. He caught two fish: one to eat, and one to be put back in the water to cheer it up, because everyone likes to feel cheerful.

When evening came he picked up his fish and his bucket, his ink and his quill pen, and the letter too, and he started for home.

Wait a minute, Little Bear! You nearly forgot your fishing rod!

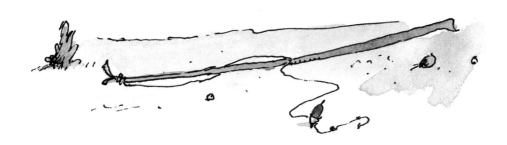

---

to stick up: zukleben
fishing rod: Angelrute

»Oh yes, so I did! Thank you very much,« says
Little Bear.
When he reached the top of the hill, he began
calling out:
»A letter! For Tiger!
A letter! For Tiger!«

But Little Tiger did not hear him. Tiger was lying
in the grass behind their little house.
He had not peeled any onions or boiled any
potatoes. He had not swept the living room floor
or watered the flowers. He had not wanted to do
anything at all, because he still felt so lonely.

And now he did not even want his letter, either.

Because Little Bear was home again himself,
in person.

That night Little Tiger woke Little Bear up.

»Listen, I must just ask you something before you
go to sleep,« he said. »Could you send your letter
rather earlier tomorrow? Perhaps you could send it
by express messenger.«

»All right,« said Little Bear, and next day he took
all his things out with him again. The ink, the quill
pen, notepaper, and an envelope.

---

express messenger: schneller Bote

But today he took a stamp too.

Down by the riverside, he put the worm on the
hook and he put the hook and line in the water
again. Then he wrote:
»Dear Tiger,
please do all the things I asked you to do when I
wrote yesterday. I hope you are well. In haste!
With lots of love and kisses from Little Bear.«
Then the elegant goose came by.

»Could you deliver my letter, please? It's for my friend Tiger, at home.«
»So sorry,« said the elegant goose. »I'm in a dreadful hurry. I have to attend a funeral.«

---

funeral: Beerdigung

Then the fat fish came by.
»Could you deliver my letter, please? It's
for - « But the fish had shot off again already.
Fishes are quick movers.
And perhaps hard of hearing, too.

---

to shoot off: davonflitzen

Then the mouse came running by, very light on her
feet.
Yes, she said, she would deliver the letter. But along
came a little blue wind. It filled out the letter like a
sail, and it almost blew letter and mouse and all away.

Then the fox came by.
»Could you deliver my letter, please, Mr Fox?«
asked Little Bear.
»It's for my friend Tiger, at home.«

»Your friend Tiger, at home?« said the fox.
»So sorry, I can't spare the time. I have to attend the
elegant goose's funeral with her.«

Life is short, little goose!
Then the elephant came by, in his boat.

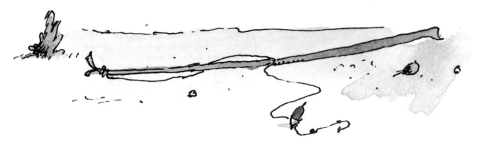

»Hi! Elephant!« shouted Little Bear.
»Come here! Listen!«
But the elephant must have been asleep, because he
did not move.

The donkey with the rucksack on his back would
not deliver the letter either.
Nor would the little man with the long nose.

But then the hare came by, wearing his fast running
shoes. »Mr Bear, give me your letter! It will get there all
the better. Stamp it, then your job is done.«
Now run, hare, run, hare, run! And the hare ran as fast as
the wind, as fast as lightning, as fast as his shoes would
carry him. He ran to Little Tiger, at home.

Little Tiger had not felt like doing anything that day either. He had not peeled any onions or boiled any potatoes. He had not swept the living room floor. He had not even lit the stove.

»A letter for Tiger!« cried the fast hare, and Little
Tiger jumped up and shouted:
»Where, why, what, when? Who's it for and who's
it from?«
»It's for Tiger,« said the hare.
»Oh well, I'm Tiger myself, so hand it over!«
Tiger danced for joy. He danced on the table,
he danced on the chair, he danced on the bed and
he danced on the sofa. He read the letter from
beginning to end, and then he read it from end
to beginning.

He felt like doing all sorts of things now.
He peeled the onions and boiled the potatoes.
He swept the floor. Life was good. He lit a nice hot
fire in the stove, and picked parsley in the garden
to go with the delicious fish they would have for
supper.

———

parsley: Petersilie

And when Little Bear came home, they spent a cosy evening together. They had fish and hot potatoes for supper, and they drank spring water from the well.

After their nice supper, they had a lovely time dancing and singing and playing music. One of the two friends played the wooden-spoon-fiddle, and Tiger played the broomstick-double-bass.

Far away, the happy mole heard the beautiful music, and he came to visit them at once.

He danced a romantic waltz with his walking stick, on the table.

---

wooden-spoon-fiddle: Kochlöffelgeige
broomstick-double-bass: Besenstielbass

»This is the happiest day of my whole life,«
said Little Tiger.
And that was no lie.

That night, Little Tiger woke Little Bear up. »There's something I just wanted to tell you before you go to sleep,« he said. »*You* can get the letter tomorrow, to cheer you up too! A letter for me one day, and a letter for you the next. Good night!«

Next day, Little Tiger took his basket for gathering mushrooms, and the bottle of blue ink and the canary quill and the notepaper, and he went out into the wood.

mushrooms: Pilze

It was *his* turn to write Little Bear a letter today.
He wrote:
»Dear Friend Little Bear,
I am writing you a letter so as to cheer you up.
I hope we shall meet again soon. This evening there
will be mushrooms for supper ... mushrooms

stewed in butter. I can see them growing
close to me here. With love and kisses from
your affectionate friend Tiger.
P.S. Wait for me.«

And so it went on, day after day. One day Little
Bear wrote to Little Tiger, and the next day Little
Tiger wrote to Little Bear. The fast hare was their
postman.

One night, Little Tiger woke Little Bear up.
»Listen,« he said, »why don't we write Auntie
Goose a letter some day? That would cheer her up,
too. All right?«
So they wrote their Auntie Goose a letter the very
next day. They sent her lots of love and kisses, and
hoped she was well, and so on.

---

affectionate: gütig, herzlich

Then Auntie Goose wrote to her Cousin
Hedgehog.
And Cousin Hedgehog wrote to the little man with
the long nose.

The elephant wanted to write to his wife in Africa.
»I can't go all the way to Africa,« said the fast hare.
»That's air mail. The carrier pigeon takes air mail
letters.«

---

carrier pigeon: Brieftaube

Now that everyone was writing letters, the fast hare could not deliver them all by himself. He asked the other hares who lived in the wood to come and be postmen too.

»You must be very fast, and very discreet,« he said. »You mustn't read the letters, and you mustn't tell anyone what's in them, understand?«

»We understand,« said the hares in their fast running shoes, and sure enough, they all understood.

Boxes were hung on all the trees, to take the letters, so that the hares would not have to call on everyone to fetch them. The boxes were painted yellow.

---

discreet: verschwiegen
to call on everyone: bei jedem vorbeigehen

One day Little Tiger said, »You know, Little Bear, when you're in the living room and I'm in the kitchen, I still feel lonely.«
So they got the garden hose and laid it between the two rooms. Now they had a telephone in their house. »Can you hear me? Hullo, hullo! Can you hear me? Who is it speaking?«

»It's Mr Bear speaking, and I can hear you loud and clear.«

»You know what?« said Little Tiger. »We could lay a telephone line in the river too. Then I wouldn't have to work so hard at writing letters the whole time.«

So that was what they did. They laid an underwater cable.

»Suppose we had a telephone line like that under the ground?« said Little Tiger. »Then we could ring up Auntie Goose on the other side of the wood.«

So the moles dug them an underground telephone system. The lines went from here to there and from hither to thither, in fact all over the place.

»Hullo, Auntie Goose, this is Little Tiger.
Can you hear me, Auntie Goose? Yes, it's me!
Lit-tle Ti-ger! The one with the little stripy tail behind him. Your nephew!«
»And this is Little Bear,« said Little Bear.
»Tell her I'm here too, Tiger!«

---

from hither to thither: kreuz und quer

The elephant phoned the telephone exchange.
»Operator speaking! Operator speaking! Africa?
No, I'm sorry, we have no lines to Africa.
Goodbye.«
»Oh well,« said the elephant, »never mind.
I'll write an air mail letter instead.«

---

telephone exchange: Vermittlung

And now everyone who lived in the wood or
by the riverside could write letters to everyone else,
and you could ring up your girl friend long
distance if you liked.
Wasn't that wonderful?

»Oh, Bear,« said Little Tiger. »I do think life is
tremendously good, don't you?«
»Yes,« said Little Bear. »Tremendous *and* good.«

And if you ask me, they were quite right.

---

tremendously: unheimlich

In der Reihe
MINIMAX
liegen folgende fremdsprachige Titel vor:

Helme Heine

Friends
(Englische Ausgabe von
Freunde)

Trois amis
(Französische Ausgabe von
Freunde)

Üç Arkadaş
(Türkische Ausgabe von
Freunde)

Janosch

A Letter for Tiger
(Englische Ausgabe von
Post für den Tiger)

Little Tiger, Get Well Soon!
(Englische Ausgabe von
*Ich mach dich gesund, sagte
der Bär*)

The Trip to Panama
(Englische Ausgabe von
Oh, wie schön ist Panama)